Saint Jenni
Chilling Out

Doctor, racing driver, ballerina, space explorer –
everyone wants to do something exciting when
they grow up. Including Jenni. She's aiming for
the top. Jenni wants to be – a saint!

Right now, Jenni wants to live a simple life;
she's going to chill out and be calm like St Teresa.
Boring? Far from it! There are accidents in the
garden, alarms in the night, agonies over the
school play and really bad hair days. As if that's
not enough, how do you stay cool when your best
friend stomps off in a huff?

Meg Harper combines writing with teaching
drama. In her spare time she enjoys swimming,
walking her dog, reading and visiting tea shops.
Her website is at www.megharper.co.uk.

Other titles in this series:

Saint Jenni: Animal Crazy
Saint Jenni: Super Hero

For Peter,
with love and thanks

Chilling Out

Meg Harper

Illustrations by Jan McCafferty

LION
CHILDREN'S

A Lion Children's Book
an imprint of
Lion Hudson plc
Mayfield House, 256 Banbury Road,
Oxford OX2 7DH, England
www.lionhudson.com
ISBN 0 7459 4896 0

First edition 2005
10 9 8 7 6 5 4 3 2 1 0

Typeset in 13.5/19 Baskerville MT Schoolbook
Printed and bound in Great Britain
by Cox and Wyman Ltd, Reading

Contents

1

A touch of the sun

'Now dear, what do you want to do when you grow up?' asked Great-Aunt Bertha at long last. Frankly, I think being made to visit old aunts is cruelty to children. Kids aren't meant to sit quietly for hours. Boring or what?

I suppose it could have been worse. At least Great-Aunt Bertha hadn't said, 'My how you've grown!' like people usually do. I smiled politely.

'When I grow up, I want to be a saint,' I said. 'I'm already in training.'

Dad groaned. 'Oh, Jenni, not that old rubbish again! I thought you'd grown out of that!'

Mum looked apologetic. 'It's since she started reading that *Big Book of Saints* that her grandpa left for her. She's got really obsessed by it.'

'I remember,' said Great-Aunt Bertha. 'He showed it to me before he died. It's a beautiful book.' She turned to me. 'Your grandpa was my brother, you know – well, of course you do, a bright spark like you. He'd have been thrilled that you like the book so much. But wanting to be a saint! That's a bit tough, isn't it? A lot of them got killed, you know.'

'Lots didn't, though,' I said, delighted that she was showing an interest – unlike some people I have to live with (three letters, begins with D and ends with D). 'But it *is* hard work. I tried training to be a saint who's good with animals and I was hopeless – but the vicar did give me my lovely kitten, Halo. And I tried being the sort of saint who does daring deeds...'

'And that was disastrous!' interrupted Mum. 'She tried to steal the church brasses and we had the police round. Another time she got a terrible cut on her head and then she nearly drowned rescuing Halo from the river!'*

* See *Saint Jenni: Super Hero*

'I didn't nearly drown,' I argued. 'I can swim now, remember?'

Great-Aunt Bertha was chuckling. 'Well, it sounds very exciting to me! What sort of saint are you going to try being next?'

'Don't encourage her, *please!*' groaned Dad.

'Oh you are dull, Jeff!' said Great-Aunt Bertha and I'm sure she winked at me. 'At least you haven't got a daughter who does nothing but watch television. How about trying some of the quieter saints, for a change?'

'That sounds nice,' said Mum.

'Quieter? How d'you mean?' I asked.

'Oh, the ones who prayed a lot or shut themselves away from the world...'

'Sounds a bit boring,' I said.

'Hmm... you'd be surprised,' said Great-Aunt Bertha with a twinkle in her eye. 'But there *are* others – ones who founded schools and hospitals, ones who lived very simple lives, ones who loved music and flowers...'

'Ones who loved music and flowers?' said

Mum. 'That sounds fairly harmless. Who were they?'

'I know! I know!' I butted in. 'St Cecilia is the musical one and St Dorothy is something to do with flowers.'

'St Dorothy?' asked Great-Aunt Bertha. 'I was thinking of Hildegard of Bingen.'

'What a name!' said Dad. 'Sounds like a right old battle-axe to me.'

'Oh, she was certainly a strong character,' said Great-Aunt Bertha. 'Isn't she in your book, Jenni?'

I nodded. 'She is,' I said. 'But the picture's just a nun in a garden.'

'Well, go and read about her,' said my great-aunt. 'Her story's more interesting than you think.'

Great-Aunt Bertha was right. Hildegard of Bingen *was* very interesting. She believed God started speaking to her when she was only three years old! And when she became a nun she was only a teenager! Later she wrote books about God. But the most interesting thing was that, even though she lived hundreds of years ago, she cared about pollution and people spoiling the earth. Maybe that was because she was a very keen gardener. Next day, I told Mum about her.

'Well, she was quite right,' said Mum. 'And we do our best. We recycle as much as we can and we make compost. I go to work on my bike so we only need one car and we *always* re-use our carrier bags. We may not be saints but we do try.'

'I know *you* do,' I said, 'but I was wondering what *I* could do. Maybe I could try some gardening? My name *is* Jenni Gardner after all.'

Mum looked panic-stricken. She's very proud of the garden. It's only small but it's beautiful. She absolutely loves all those gardening programmes.

'Err... I don't know what you could do really, love. I try to keep on top of the work myself.' She looked guilty – and so she should. There's me trying to be helpful in the garden and she won't let me! What sort of parent is that?

Suddenly, Mum's face lit up. 'I'll tell you what,' she said. 'Why don't you ask the vicar? He's got a huge garden. Maybe he'd be glad of some help. And he did give you Halo. It'd be a nice way of saying thank you.'

I considered it. She certainly had a point. At that moment, Halo herself wandered in and wrapped herself round my legs. 'Miaow,' she said. It seemed like a sign – so I went to see the vicar.

'Why, hello Jenni!' he said. 'How's my favourite saint-in-training?'

'That's what I've come to see you about,' I said. 'I've been reading about Hildegard of Bingen so I wondered if you wanted any help with your garden.'

'I'm sorry? I'm not sure I understand.'

Patiently, I explained. It's remarkable how little he knows about saints, considering he's a vicar.

'Well,' he said. 'This isn't the best day, actually,

Jenni. We've got visitors, and with it being Sunday I'm quite busy.'

'But it's such lovely weather for gardening,' I said. 'And I'll be at school tomorrow.'

He was weakening, I could see. He's always so kind.

'I won't be any trouble,' I said. 'You just show me a patch that needs weeding and I'll get on with it.'

'Hmm...' said the vicar. 'Do you know much about gardening?'

Saints don't do lying so I was very careful what I said. 'Quite a bit,' I told him. 'Mum's always talking about it.'

'Well, I don't suppose it matters much,' he said. 'Our garden's such a mess anyway. Come on. I'm sure no one will mind if you get on with a bit of quiet weeding.'

He led me through the house and out of the back door.

His visitors were sitting around a big table on the patio. They'd obviously just finished lunch.

'Won't be a minute!' called the vicar, and he led me down the side of the lawn and into a part of the garden which had been left to go wild.

'This is the old kitchen garden,' he said. 'I'm trying to grow a few things but I'm not getting very far, as you can see.'

There was one small area that had been cleared, where a few things were growing.

'It looks very promising,' I said, like my mum does when she's being encouraging. The vicar looked depressed.

'Well, I do try,' he said with a sigh. 'It'd be great to eat a few home-grown things, wouldn't it? I'm sure your Hilda of Wotsit would approve of that, wouldn't she? But I'm so busy.'

'It's Hildegard of Bingen,' I said. 'And I'm here to help – so soon you should have lots of home-grown things to eat.'

The vicar smiled. 'That would be really lovely,' he said. 'If you need any tools, they're in that little shed. Now I'm afraid I really must get back to my visitors.'

'That's fine,' I said. 'You just have a nice afternoon.'

I got a big fork from the shed and chose a particularly weedy patch of ground to start on. I knew that it would need a good digging but first I had to get the weeds out. The soil was very dry and hard but once I'd got the fork in, the weeds came up fairly easily.

At first it was fun. The sun was warm on my back and bees were buzzing happily from plant to plant. There was no breeze and the scents of summer filled the air. Hildegard used to kneel down among her plants so she could touch them and breathe in their perfumes. I tried it myself. It was lovely. Even weeds smell wonderfully green. I brushed the leaves against my face, just like Hildegard in the picture in my book. She even used to nibble her plants to get to know them better. I nibbled a few myself – not many, of course. I know that some plants are poisonous but I didn't think the vicar would have any, not with three small children around. But I only ate a very little – just to be on the safe side. They tasted... well... green is probably the best word.

As I carried on digging, it got hotter and hotter and harder and harder work. The sun was beating down on me and I was getting very sweaty and thirsty. But I didn't want to disturb the vicar and I didn't want to stop. My cleared patch seemed very small. Maybe I could get a drink from a garden tap somewhere. Then I saw something else. Lettuces.

Some kids don't like lettuce, but I do. It's nicest in a salad with honey and mustard dressing – yum! – but I don't mind it on its own. And the vicar's lettuces looked so fresh and green and thirst-quenching. I was sure he wouldn't mind if I ate just one – he's such a kind man.

I crouched down and pulled off an outer leaf. Maybe that would do. I shook off the dirt and flicked away a couple of creepy-crawlies, then crammed it into my mouth. Mmm. Not exactly delicious but definitely better than nothing. I took another leaf and another and another. By then the lettuce looked like it had been attacked by monster slugs so I pulled the rest of it up, broke off the root and crammed the leaves into my mouth. That was better. I could manage a bit more weeding now.

Then I noticed the strawberries. They grow very close to the ground and I hadn't spotted them before. There were lots of pale ones, not quite ripe – in a few days, the vicar would have loads. I was sure he wouldn't mind if I took a few of the red ones. It wouldn't be stealing – just a little payment for the work I'd done – and anyway, if I left them, the slugs would only eat them.

I crouched down again and plucked a big, juicy strawberry. Mmm! It was heavenly – the scent was fantastic and it tasted blissful. The juice was so refreshing that I took another… and another. Soon, there were no red ones left. But there were plenty of pale ones. The vicar wouldn't mind. He would have bucketfuls. And now I could get on with some more weeding.

But when I stood up, I felt dizzy. Suddenly, my head began to pound. I staggered and clutched at the fork which I'd left sticking in the ground. I felt really ill! What was happening to me? I'd been hot and clammy before but now I began to shake. I couldn't focus; the garden seemed to swim before my eyes. Surely those weeds I'd nibbled couldn't have poisoned me? But maybe they had! Or maybe the vicar had put slug-killer on his strawberries and lettuces? Could that kill you? How could I have been so stupid?

I began to weave my way back towards the house. I staggered out onto the lawn.

'Help!' I called, feebly, my knees beginning to buckle. 'Help!'

Through a blur, I could see the people at the garden table jumping up. The vicar came rushing over. He grabbed my shoulders. 'Jenni,' he shouted, his voice seeming to come from a long way off. 'Jenni! What's the matter?'

'I… I…' I wanted to tell him about the lettuce and the strawberries. If I was going to die, I wanted to say sorry. Suddenly it seemed quite wrong to have eaten them. Not the sort of thing a trainee saint should do at all. 'I'm s… s… sorry,' I stuttered. 'I ate the…' And then everything was fuzzy and my head was pounding too much for me to carry on.

I was very sick in the ambulance. I can remember that. And feeling very, very tired.

When I woke up, Mum was gazing down at me. I felt hot but there was something wonderfully cool and soothing on my head.

'Oh Jenni,' said Mum and her voice cracked. 'You had us worried to death.'

'Where am I?' I mumbled.

'Hospital. The vicar thought you'd eaten something poisonous. The doctor thinks it's heat exhaustion but they've kept you here for observation. I need to tell someone you've woken up.'

I felt very peculiar indeed. When the nurse

came, she made me drink some water and told me to keep drinking as much as I could. It was an effort just to lift the beaker.

At last, after I'm sure I'd drunk enough water to fill a swimming pool, the doctor said I could go home.

'No more playing in the sun without a hat, a drink and your sunscreen, young lady,' he said, glaring at Mum, who went very red indeed. 'And certainly no more eating plants!'

'I was *gardening*, not playing,' I told him, 'and it was only a little nibble.'

'Even a little nibble can be serious,' he said, 'so don't argue. Anyway, you're obviously much better so off you go.'

Poor Mum felt really bad. She said she'd been so worried about me wrecking her garden that all the sensible stuff about being in the sun went right out of her head. She rang the vicar to apologize but sent me round the next day. I took Halo with me. I needed her support. It's hard, saying sorry to a vicar for eating all his ripe strawberries – and a lettuce, of course. He made it easy though.

'Well, hello Jenni – and hello Halo,' he said. 'I suppose you've come to say sorry for scaring me to death and eating all my ripe strawberries?'

'And one of your lettuces,' I said.

'Not one of my lettuces as well!' He held up his hands in horror. 'I thought that was the slugs.'

'Just one very big slug,' I said. 'I'm really sorry.'

'Well, I forgive you,' he said. 'Just don't do it again. I must have aged about ten years. Just imagine the headlines. CHILD POISONED IN VICAR'S GARDEN.'

I grinned. 'I don't suppose you'll want me to help any more,' I said.

'Oh yes I do!' he said. 'I think this Hildegard of Bingen was onto something. We don't spend enough time caring for the wonderful things God has made. Gardening would be good for us both – but next time, I shall keep an eye on you! All right?'

'All right,' I said, 'but you don't need to worry

about your strawberries. I've gone right off them.'

'What about my lettuces?'

I smiled. 'I prefer them with honey and mustard dressing,' I said.

2

Anyone for a garden make-over?

The vicar and I have really taken to gardening. I go round a couple of times a week. One of us plays with his kids while the other one does some gardening. It works really well! Things are definitely beginning to grow. One day the vicar said to me, 'You know, Jenni, sometimes when I'm here, just quietly digging, I wish I was one of those saints who went off and lived in a hut on their own somewhere.'

'Like St Simeon or St Cuthbert?' I said.

'Maybe. I don't remember the names. I just like the idea of being somewhere peaceful to think and pray.'

I nodded. 'It would be lovely,' I agreed. 'No school, no jobs, no Mum nagging me to tidy my room. I could just chill out. It'd be brilliant.'

The vicar laughed. 'I don't think saints *just* chill out, Jenni,' he said. 'I think there's a bit more to it than that.'

That night, I got out my *Big Book of Saints* again. I'd decided to find out about the very quiet saints – but I didn't get past St Teresa of Avila. She had some cool ideas. When she was a kid, she and her brother tried to make caves so they could live like hermits. When she got older she lived a really simple life – she slept on straw, didn't eat meat and didn't wear shoes. It sounded lovely, like in the story of Heidi when she slept in the hay and ran around the mountain barefoot. But I liked the cave idea best. St Teresa's fell down but with a bit of planning, I didn't see why mine should.

The next Saturday afternoon, Mum had to go shopping and Dad was keen to watch a big football match on TV. I said I'd be all right just playing on my own. Mum looked worried.

'Are you sure?' she said. 'I don't want you getting into trouble. And remember, if you go outside, wear your hat, put on your sunscreen and have plenty to drink.'

'I will,' I said. 'I'm not stupid.'

Secretly, I couldn't wait for Mum to go. This was the perfect chance to make my cave.

For years, there's been a pile of rocks in the corner of our garden. Mum didn't seem to want them for anything and they looked just right for my cave!

There was an old bag of cement in the shed and I reckoned that if I used that, my cave would stand up far better than St Teresa's. I'd be doing everyone a favour. Mum keeps nagging Dad to get rid of the cement because it's in the way. Also, just the other weekend, she dragged me round this fancy garden and went on and on about how lovely this thing called The Hermit's Rustic Cave was. Well, now she could have her very own Hermit's Rustic Cave in the garden –

instead of an old pile of rocks in the corner. And I could use it for training to be a chilled-out saint! Perfect!

I put on my sunscreen and my hat, drank some water and got started. The instructions on the cement seemed straightforward. They said I had to add sand to make mortar so I shovelled some out of my old sandpit. Mum's been dying to get rid of it so I was sure that would be OK. They also said I had to wear gloves so I found a pair of Mum's. I mixed in some water with an old wooden spoon I'd found in the kitchen. The mortar was a bit runny so I added some more sand. Then it was a bit stiff so I added more water. In the end, I had a whole bucketful. Plenty for a small cave, I thought.

It was hard work, moving the rocks, but before too long I had quite a big pile ready. I stood some of them close together in a ring with a space for the entrance, then slopped some mortar in the gaps. That looked quite good, so I started on the second layer. That was when it got tricky. The rocks were all different shapes and fitting them together was hard. I managed it in the end and stood back to look at my work. It wasn't bad. The mortar was beginning to dry and it looked pretty solid. The third layer was going to be difficult, though; the mortar left in the bucket was beginning to set. I would have to work fast.

Just then Mum returned from her shopping trip. The time had flown. When she saw my half-finished cave, her jaw dropped.

'What on earth is that?' she gasped.

'It's my hermit's cave,' I said. It did look a bit strange and lopsided but then so had the Hermit's Rustic Cave. 'Don't worry,' I added, 'it'll look great when it's finished. Just like the one we saw in that posh garden – and it'll be perfect for doing saint training.'

'In the middle of my lawn?' said Mum.

I was puzzled. 'Why not?' I said. 'It's a special feature.'

'Where did you get the stones from?' demanded

Mum. I could see she wasn't impressed at all.

'In the corner,' I said. 'You didn't seem to want them. And I used up the old cement and the sand from my sandpit. Don't worry, I followed the instructions, but I'd better get on with it because the mortar is setting.'

'You mean you've cemented my rocks together?' said Mum. She had gone all pale and funny-looking. 'In the middle of my lawn? When I was saving them for a rockery? And you've made mortar in my new bucket? Don't tell me that's my mum's old wooden spoon! It's my favourite for making sauces!'

I hid my hands behind my back. Her gloves were plastered with mortar and, for all I knew, they were extra special too!

'Really Jenni!' Mum looked as if she was going to cry. 'I *told* you I didn't want you getting into trouble!'

'But I...'

'Don't try to explain! Just go and get yourself cleaned up! Jeff! Jeff! Come out here this minute!

Can't you be trusted to keep an eye on Jenni for even a couple of hours?'

And she went stomping off into the house to find Dad.

Well! You just can't please some people, can you? How was I to know she was saving the rocks for a rockery? They've been there forever! Or that it was a new bucket or her special spoon? And how was I to know that Mum wouldn't want her very own Hermit's Rustic Cave? I thought it would be a nice surprise!

Worst of all, after all that work I'd done, Mum made Dad pull it all apart before the mortar set completely. He couldn't do the bottom layer and had to ask our neighbour Mr Brindley if he could borrow a big mallet. Mrs Brindley asked if I'd like to come round to her house, seeing as I might be in the way. I shot round there like a bullet from a gun! I did *not* want to stay while Dad wrecked my cave or listen to Mum going on about how thoughtless I'd been. I knew Mrs Brindley would understand; she likes stories about saints too.

Sometimes I wonder how I'd manage without her and the vicar.

'I was trying to be helpful,' I wailed. 'And Mum thought it would be *nice* if I tried being a quiet saint for a change!'

'I'm sure it would, Jenni,' said Mrs Brindley, giving me a glass of juice and two chocolate biscuits. 'The problem is trying to think things through from every point of view. Your mum might like a Hermit's Rustic Cave as something to go and visit – but not in the middle of her very small lawn. And not made out of the rocks she was saving.'

I sighed. 'I suppose so,' I said. 'I suppose I should have asked her first. I just thought it would be a nice surprise.'

'And a nice cave for you too?' asked Mrs Brindley, with a smile.

'Well, yes, that as well,' I admitted. Saints do have to be very honest.

'I'm sure you don't have to actually live in a cave to be saintly,' said Mrs Brindley. 'Maybe you could live a simple life in a different way? Why don't you have a think about that?'

I pulled a face. 'I'll try,' I said, 'but I don't feel very much like training to be a saint any more. Everything I do seems to go wrong.'

'Oh Jenni!' said Mrs Brindley. 'That's a shame. I know you've had a few disasters but I really admire the way you keep on trying.'

'Would you like to be a saint too then?' I asked, in surprise.

'No, but I'd certainly like to be a bit more saintly,' said Mrs Brindley. 'I'm not always as nice as you think I am. I need someone to spur me on!'

'Well, I guess I'll keep trying then,' I said. I really like Mrs Brindley and I didn't want to let her down. 'Saints don't do giving up, do they?'

'No, I don't think so,' said Mrs Brindley. 'But I think they choose very carefully what they *do* do, all right?'

I'd finished my drink and biscuits so I said goodbye and walked home. I crept upstairs and found Halo lounging on my bed.

'Oh Halo,' I said sadly, picking her up and cuddling her. 'It certainly isn't easy training to be a saint.' I looked at my *Big Book of Saints* which was lying on the floor. For the first time ever, in spite of what Mrs Brindley had said, I wished I'd never started reading it.

3

Noises in the night

The next morning, I still felt glum. I think Mum felt bad about how angry she'd been.

'Cheer up, Jenni love,' she said over breakfast. 'I'm sure trainee saints aren't meant to look quite so miserable.'

'I'm not sure I want to be a saint any more,' I said. 'Everything I try to do goes wrong.'

'Oh,' said Mum, looking a bit shocked. 'Oh dear, I'd feel really bad if you gave up.'

'What?' I said. 'But you think it's silly to want to be a saint!'

'Well…' said Mum, 'it did seem strange at first – I mean, we don't even go to church – but a lot of good has come from the things you've done.'

I was stunned. 'Like what?' I said. 'I can't think of *anything*!'

'Oh Jenni, you *are* in a bad mood!' said Mum. 'You've got Halo for a start – no one else wanted her! And then there's Daisy. She was really lonely before you made friends with her.'

'Yes, but…' I interrupted.

'Never mind "yes, but"! Then there're those girls, Jade and Shelley. The other mums say they're much better-behaved now, thanks to you. You're helping the vicar with his garden – and you've learnt to swim!* You may never be a saint, but you've achieved a lot just by trying!'

'Wow!' I said. 'It does sound pretty amazing when you put it like that.'

'It *is* amazing,' said Mum. 'It makes me very proud of you and pretty ashamed that I haven't been much help.'

'That's OK,' I said. 'Saints often had to do things on their own.'

Mum smiled. 'That's more like it!' she said.

* See *Saint Jenni: Animal Crazy* and *Saint Jenni: Super Hero*

'But I would like to do something to help – so I wondered if you'd like me to buy you a little tent.'

'A little tent? What for?'

'Well,' said Mum, 'if you really want somewhere to be on your own, a little tent might be the very thing. They don't cost very much. What d'you think?'

A tent – of my very own! Brilliant! I didn't actually know of a saint who lived in a tent, though St Paul used to make them – but I could see what Mum meant. Cheap – well, cheapish – and simple. Fantastic!

'It sounds ace!' I said. 'When can we get one?'

Mum took me shopping the very next day. We chose a one-person tent – nothing bigger would fit on the lawn – but we reckoned there was room for both Daisy and me when I wasn't being quiet and chilled.

That week was warm and sunny and I spent most of the evenings curled up in my tent with Halo, my books and my MP3 player. I remembered what the vicar said about saints not *just* chilling out so I tried to do some praying. I managed about five minutes each day. Mrs Brindley said it didn't matter if you started small.

On Friday evening, Daisy came round to play.

'Oh, this tent is lovely!' she sighed, as she lay down inside it. 'Wouldn't it be fantastic to sleep out here?'

'What? On our own?' I said.

'Yes! We could pretend we were saints who wanted to get really close to nature.'

'You mean like St Sergius or St Francis? Or Hildegard of Bingen?'

'Probably. I don't know the names.' Her eyes had gone all starry. 'Ooh, wouldn't it be great? Why don't we ask your mum if we can do it tomorrow?'

'But...' I said and then stopped. How could I explain to Daisy that the very idea scared me stiff? Sleep outside on our own? Was she mad? Anything could happen to us! The trouble was that I used to think Daisy was a wimp. She cried a lot. Now I know she was miserable because she didn't have any friends and her mum has this thing called MS which makes her very poorly. Daisy's very careful about keeping clean and that sort of thing because she doesn't want to make extra work for her mum. She has cute little bunches, and round cheeks like a guinea pig, but she can be much more daring than me. I didn't want her thinking *I* was a wimp – especially since sometimes saints have to be very brave.

'OK then,' I said. 'Let's go and ask Mum. But she'll probably say no. She's so proud of her garden.'

But she didn't. 'What a super idea!' she said. 'I'll phone Daisy's mum straight away and see what she thinks.'

I gulped. 'Are you sure it'll be safe?' I asked. 'I'm trying to think of things from every point of view. Saints have to do that.'

'Safe?' said Mum. 'Of course it will. We don't have a back gate to our garden and you can borrow my mobile and ring us if there's a problem. But there won't be. You'll be fine!'

I wasn't so sure. I worried all the next day until Daisy arrived. After that, we had a great time. Dad did a barbecue and we toasted marshmallows. Then we went inside and made fantastic cocktails, mixing fizzy water, juice and chopped-up fruit. Mum even found some of those little paper parasols to put in the top and showed us how to frost the rims of the glasses with sugar. It was a very warm evening, so we laid out a rug in front of the tent and lounged around, sipping our drinks and nibbling peanuts.

It was only when it began to get dark that I started getting nervous. Even though ours is such a small garden, I didn't like it when I couldn't see into the corners any more.

'Let's get ready for bed now,' I said. 'I'm getting cold.' Really, I wanted to be inside the tent; I'd feel a bit safer in there.

'Fine,' said Daisy. 'D'you think we could make some hot chocolate first?'

I jumped at the idea. Anything to get us back inside the house! Then Mum suggested we had our drinks in the tent.

'But we might spill them,' I said. 'We might trip up in the dark.'

'Oh, don't be silly,' said Mum. 'It'll be so cosy, tucked up inside your tent with your hot chocolate. I'll bring it out in a minute.'

Gloomily, I followed Daisy back out to the tent. Halo was prowling round the garden and I called to her. She always sleeps on my bed and I was sure I'd feel much better once she was snuggled in next to me.

But Halo didn't want to come to bed right then. She was busy learning to hunt.

'What if she doesn't come in later?' I said anxiously. 'She'll miss me.'

'So?' said Daisy. 'Just go and get her. And if she doesn't come, well, it's only for one night. She'll be all right.'

I started chewing my nails. It wasn't Halo I was worried about! Go and get her? Creep across the garden with only a torch for a light? No way! But I couldn't imagine getting to sleep without her. I'd be terrified.

'What if we want to go to the loo in the night?' I said.

'Jenni, what's the matter with you?' said Daisy. 'Just go. We've got torches.'

I'd been hoping Daisy would suggest that we went together; I was too embarrassed to suggest it myself. The night stretched ahead of me like a horrible, dark tunnel. I'd be lying awake with no Halo to cuddle, frightened and desperate to go to the loo. I put my mug down, regretting all the drinks I'd had. This was going to be a nightmare.

At first, it wasn't too bad. We played cards for ages, told jokes and got the giggles. Then Mum came out and told us to settle down. I rushed in with Mum to go to the loo and look for Halo but I couldn't find her anywhere.

'Hurry up, Jenni,' said Mum, standing by the door and looking stern. 'Halo can look after herself. Now I want to see those torches go off!'

Within minutes, Daisy was fast asleep while I lay on my back, trying to relax but jumping at every sound. I couldn't believe how *noisy* the garden was. The night was very still and I'm sure I could even hear the ants scuttling around. After what felt like hours, I was worn out with listening. There were plenty of saints who didn't think anything of staying awake all night praying but I'd had enough – so I tried a different sort of prayer.

'Dear God,' I whispered, 'please help me not to be scared and to go to sleep quickly. Amen.'

Then I shut my eyes, curled up as small as I could and put my fingers in my ears.

The prayer must have worked because the next thing I knew, I was sitting bolt upright in my sleeping bag, screaming!

'Help me! Help me! It's got me!' I was yelling, or so Daisy told me later. 'Go away, go away! Don't touch me!'

'Jenni, be quiet, it's me, Daisy, you're all right!' Daisy shouted at me, grabbing my shoulders and trying to get me to lie down.

'Get off me! Get off me!' I carried on shrieking. 'Leave me alone! Help! Mummy! Daddy!'

Dad struggled through the tent-door, calling my name.

'Jenni love, it's me, Daddy. You're all right, I'm here now.'

Then he bundled me against him, sleeping bag and all, and started rocking me like a baby, muttering, 'There, there, it's all right, love. It was just a bad dream.' Daisy started stroking my arm and saying, 'There, there' too! Embarrassing or what?

'It was Halo,' said Daisy, when we were all sitting in the kitchen recovering with more hot chocolate.

'Halo? What d'you mean?' asked Mum. Halo was sitting on my lap, purring fit to bust.

'She jumped on top of the tent. She must have leapt from the fence or something. She didn't half give me a fright – but she must have turned into a nightmare for Jenni.'

'I knew I should have found her before I went to bed,' I said. 'I really wanted to.'

'It wasn't your fault,' said Mum. 'It was such a nice evening, she could have been streets away. Anyway, we'd better get back to bed…'

Just at that moment, the doorbell rang.

'Good heavens, who can that be?' said Dad. 'It's four o'clock in the morning!'

'Oh dear, maybe it's one of the neighbours complaining,' said Mum.

'I can't imagine who,' said Dad as he hurried to the door.

It wasn't a neighbour, it was the police.

'There's been a report of a disturbance,' said the policeman on the doorstep. 'We're just making a few enquiries. Have you been disturbed at all tonight, sir?'

'Mm… I think you'd better come in,' said Dad, sounding embarrassed. 'I think we may have caused the disturbance, actually.'

The policeman was very nice about it. 'Quite understandable,' he said. 'Nightmares are dreadful things. The neighbour who reported it thought a child was being attacked. It's all in a night's work. But perhaps young Jenni should sleep in the house for the rest of the night? Just to be on the safe side?'

I could have hugged him!

'Is that all right, Daisy?' I said. 'Shall we sleep in the house now? Unless you want to sleep out there on your own?'

Daisy shuddered. 'No way,' she said. 'Not without you!'

I gaped at her. 'I thought you weren't scared at all!' I said.

''Course I was,' she said. 'I just didn't want to tell you. You used to think I was such a wimp.'

'But you went straight to sleep!' I protested.

'I was pretending,' admitted Daisy. 'Once it got dark, I was terrified but I didn't dare say so – not after what I'd said earlier. I wasn't even asleep when Halo jumped on the tent. Sorry.'

I beamed at her. 'So you won't mind if we spend the rest of the night in the house?'

'Of course not! I'll go and get my sleeping bag – as long as you come with me!'

'You'll be fine,' I said. 'It's nearly light now anyway.'

'Don't be a tease, Jenni,' said Mum. 'Let's all get back to bed. I'm tired out.'

We gathered together what we needed and hurried up to my bedroom. It had never seemed so cosy and safe before.

'Oh dear,' I sighed. 'Even being a quiet saint is more difficult than you'd think.'

'Don't worry,' said Daisy. 'There must be other ways to be saintly.'

'Maybe,' I said. 'But none of them is easy.'

'Who said anything about easy?' Daisy retorted.

I yawned, snuggled down and shut my eyes. I was too tired to worry about it any longer. Within moments, I was fast asleep.

4

Saints don't do kissing!

For the next few weeks, the weather was so fantastic that going to school was torture. Luckily, the teachers had come up with something to cheer us up. The summer play! Just thinking about that Monday morning when the Headmistress read out the cast-list still makes my heart go all fluttery.

'Now, children, I'm going to tell you the names of the cast for our summer play *Cinderella*,' she said at the end of assembly. 'I know you're all dying to find out, so I won't waste any more time. The part of Cinderella is to be played by Jenni Gardner in Year 4...'

I was stunned! When I'd gone to the auditions, I'd never expected to get the leading role! I'd have been quite happy to be one of the mice who pulled the coach!

'I can't believe it,' I whispered to Daisy, as we left the hall. 'Why me?'

'Because you're brilliant at acting, of course,' said Daisy. 'You're ever so good when we play "saints".'

'It's because you've got a big mouth and you're as scruffy as Cinderella,' sneered Jade, who had overheard us. 'You won't have any problem finding a costume, will you?'

I wanted to turn round and hit her but that isn't very saintly so I pretended I hadn't heard.

'Who's playing Prince Charming?' I asked Daisy. 'I wasn't paying attention.'

'Joe Mears,' said Daisy. 'He's in Year 6.'

'I know,' I said. 'He's quite nice, isn't he?'

Daisy shrugged. 'Don't know – but a lot of girls fancy him. I hope he's not a show-off.'

'You'd better hope he hasn't got bad breath,'

said Jade, who was still hanging around. 'Seeing as you'll have to kiss him.'

'Kiss him?' I said. 'Urgh! I'm not doing that. Anyway, I bet I won't have to. I'll just have to dance with him and hold hands, that's all.'

But that was where I was wrong.

The rehearsals started. It was a very serious version of *Cinderella* with hardly any jokes. The school inspectors would be in the school the week we performed. Maybe the Headmistress thought they wouldn't like any silly scenes with custard pies and sausages. Anyway, there were loads of us involved. Apart from the actors, there was a choir and a recorder group, not to mention the stage crew, the costume-makers and the ticket-sellers. It was great fun and Joe Mears was really nice. He didn't seem to mind that I was only in Year 4 and kept telling me how well I was doing. I began to think that if I did have to kiss him in front of everyone, it wouldn't be too bad.

Then disaster struck. Miss Simpson came in all

flustered one morning. She told three people off before she'd even finished marking the register. I put my hand up. It sounded to me as if a bit of saintly help was needed.

'What is it, Jenni?' she snapped.

'Excuse me, Miss,' I said in my kindest voice. 'Is something wrong? You don't seem very happy.'

I thought Miss Simpson was going to burst into tears! Then she sniffed hard and said, 'Joe Mears had a bad accident on his skateboard last night. He's broken his leg so he won't be able to play Prince Charming. I just don't know how we're going to get anybody up to his standard in time. And the school inspectors will be watching!'

I gulped. I felt like crying myself. I tried to feel sorry for Joe and Miss Simpson but right then, I just felt sorry for me! I really liked acting with Joe.

'Don't worry, Miss,' said Daisy. 'Lots of people know his lines because they hear them so often. I'm sure you'll be able to find someone.'

'Not someone as good as Joe!' I wanted to say

but I bit back the words. They wouldn't help.

'Thank you, Daisy,' said Miss Simpson with a weak smile. 'I'm sure you're right. There must be someone good enough.'

We had to go to assembly then. Jade sneaked up behind me.

'Who's not going to get to kiss Joe then?' she said. 'Bet you're fed-up. You really fancy him, don't you?'

'Don't be stupid,' I said. 'I wasn't going to have to kiss him anyway.'

'Bet you were.'

'Bet I wasn't. Now shut up!'

'Ooh! Don't get your knickers in a twist. Thought you were supposed to be a saint!'

I ignored her. It's the best thing to do with people like her. It stops you from doing something really unsaintly like kicking them.

That evening, at the rehearsal, there was a buzz of excitement. Who was going to replace Joe? We all wanted to know. When Miss Simpson walked in, everyone stopped talking at once.

'I know what you're waiting for,' she said, with an anxious smile, 'so I'll tell you straight away. Darren Bullock, I'd like you to play the part of Prince Charming instead of Joe.'

Darren Bullock! My heart sank. He was the obvious choice, of course. Very confident and a good actor. He'd had a leading role in our Christmas play. The trouble was he's a real big-head, the sort of boy who thinks anyone younger than him isn't worth speaking to. Just the thought of dancing with him made me want to throw up.

But it was all bad news that night.

'Let's get going then,' said Miss Simpson. 'There's no time to waste. Today I think we can get on to the last scene.'

It was difficult to act with Darren. Whenever he looked at me, he seemed to sneer. We struggled through the ball scene; Darren trod on my feet several times.

'Be careful,' I hissed. 'Watch what you're doing!'

'Keep your feet out of my way then,' he hissed back.

Then, when we were waiting to start the scene where Cinderella has to try on the slipper he said, 'I hope your feet don't smell. I can't stand cheesy feet.'

I felt like slapping him but I didn't. It would have been very unsaintly and he would still be horrible, just angry as well.

Finally, we reached the last scene of all, where Prince Charming asks Cinderella to marry him.

'... and now that I have found you at last, all I can say is, will you do me the honour of becoming my wife?' said Darren, as if nothing could have made him feel more sick.

'Yes,' I snapped, looking at my feet.

'No, no, no,' said Miss Simpson. 'You have to look more in love than that! Try again – and after Jenni says yes, kiss each other.'

Darren and I looked at each other.

'Yuk,' said Darren. 'She's only in Year 4.'

'I'm not kissing him,' I said. 'He's horrible.'

'It's only acting,' said Miss Simpson. 'And I'm not asking for grand passion – just a quick peck on the cheek. Just something to show you do actually like each other.'

We tried again. To be fair, Darren said his line much better, mainly because he looked over my shoulder and not at me! Then he leaned forward and kissed me on the cheek. I could hear people sniggering.

'Yuk!' I said and scrubbed at it.

'Jenni!' Miss Simpson exploded. 'Don't be such a baby! It's only a little kiss.'

I felt terrible. I didn't want Miss Simpson thinking I was pathetic but I didn't want to kiss horrible Darren Bullock either. Jade and Shelley would never let me forget it. Then I had an idea.

'I'm sorry, Miss Simpson, but saints don't do kissing,' I said.

'What? You're not still dragging saints into everything, surely?' said Miss Simpson.

'Of course,' I said. 'I'm trying to be a quiet, chilled-out saint – and they certainly didn't do

kissing. A lot of them were nuns and nuns don't get married.'

Miss Simpson looked stunned. 'Jenni, this isn't for real,' she said. 'It's only a play. Nobody thinks you're *really* in love with Darren.'

'You're trying to force me to do something I don't want to do,' I said. 'That's what people did to the saints. St Catherine, St Frideswide and St Winifride all had that problem. An emperor tried to force St Catherine to marry him, and in the end he had her head chopped off. A prince chased St Frideswide through the forest because she wasn't in love with him and when St Winifride wouldn't marry Caradoc he threw his sword at her and sliced off her head. It grew back again though.'

Darren started to laugh. 'Don't worry, Jenni,' he said. 'I'm not going to chase you through any forests for a kiss. If she's that fussed why don't we just leave it for now, Miss? As long as she promises to do it on the night.'

'Well, Jenni?' said Miss Simpson. 'I think we've

wasted quite enough time on it for now. Can we rely on you to kiss Darren on the night? He's not that bad really, you know.'

I glowered at her. Couldn't she see that compared with Joe he was awful? 'I'll think about it,' I said.

'Good,' said Miss Simpson. 'Now let's move on.'

I did think about it, long and hard – but I still didn't know what to do. Daisy thought I was making a fuss about nothing and I didn't want to ask Mrs Brindley. She'd either tell me to look at the other person's point of view or to pray about it. Well, I could see Miss Simpson's point of view; she just wanted a nice, happy ending to her play. And I could see Darren's point of view; he didn't want me to kiss him but he was happy to go along with it. It was only me who was being awkward. I didn't think praying would be much help. What could I say? Please God, could you arrange to break Darren's leg too? I knew that I should just give in – that was the kind, brave thing to do. But every time I thought of it, I felt sick with embarrassment.

The night before the show, I sat down on my bed with Halo on my lap. I was desperate.

'Dear God,' I said. 'I don't know if there's much you can do about this – but can you please get me out of kissing Darren Bullock? I don't mean burn the school down or anything big – just something small. I know I *should* be brave but I'm just going to be so embarrassed. Thank you. Amen.'

I waited for a good five minutes, cuddling Halo and trying to keep calm and still like a chilled-out saint so that I would hear God's voice. But I didn't. Instead, Mum shouted for me to come down to tea.

It was sausage, beans and mash, my favourite, but I'd completely lost my appetite. Lots of saints had times when they didn't eat anything so they could focus their minds on God. Not me. I just felt sick at the thought of kissing Darren Bullock.

The next day was very odd. Everyone seemed jumpy and nervous. The inspectors had been prowling round the school all week and now it was the day of our performance. Even Daisy, who's far better at being calm and chilled-out than me, was a bit edgy. She was worried that her set painting wasn't good enough and that people would be rude about it.

'I don't know what you're bothered about,' I said. 'No one's going to notice if your painting's a bit dodgy. Everyone's going to see me kiss Darren Bullock!'

'Big-head!' said Daisy. 'Who cares if you do?'

'Jade and Shelley. They're bound to go on about it.'

'Only if you take any notice. If you just ignore them, they'll soon stop.'

'Oh yeah, like you just ignored them when they were mean about your Teletubbies knickers,' I said.*

Daisy flushed. 'You know I'm not such a wimp as I was then,' she said. 'I was only trying to help.'

* See *Saint Jenni: Super Hero*

It was my turn to blush. 'Sorry,' I said. 'I know I'm making a fuss – but I can't help it.'

'Oh well,' said Daisy. 'At least it'll soon be over.'

She was right. That evening, the play whizzed by. It seemed like no time at all before we were dancing at the ball and, miracle of miracles, Darren managed not to tread on my feet! I'd sprayed my feet with body spray but Darren seemed miles away. Maybe he was too worried about kissing me to bother about my smelly feet.

Then, at last, it was the final scene. The kiss loomed ahead and I still hadn't worked out what to do.

'… and now that I have found you at last, all I can say is, will you do me the honour of becoming my wife?' said Darren, looking past my right shoulder and blushing.

There was a pause. I looked at the audience. I looked back at Darren.

'Say "yes",' he mouthed.

'No,' I said, my mouth seeming to open of its own accord. 'No, I will not marry you yet, even though you are a prince. I hardly know you. I have only met you once and all we did was dance. But you do seem quite nice. Why don't we go out for a pizza and get to know each other better?'

For one terrifying moment, there was complete silence. Darren goggled at me.

'Well?' I said. 'How about it?'

'An excellent idea,' said Darren. 'I would be delighted. Pizza Hut or Pizza Express?'

And with that, he took my hand, bowed low over it and kissed it lightly. I beamed at him, we bowed to the audience and were rewarded with thunderous applause. On the very front row, one of the inspectors stood up and actually whistled.

The curtains closed. Darren turned to me. 'Wow, Jenni, you're pretty feisty for a Year 4,' he said. 'Here comes Miss Simpson. I wonder what she's going to say about that?'

I didn't really want to know. Right then I thought I would rather be the sort of saint that the Romans threw to the lions.

5

A really bad hair day

It wasn't as bad as I thought. Luckily, before Miss Simpson had a chance to chew me over and spit out the bits, the inspectors got hold of her. They adored the play – the number of children who were involved, the exciting way we'd staged it, the enthusiasm with which we took part; but most of all, they loved the surprise ending! They thought it was very modern and would make people think. I agree. It *is* a better ending. I mean, would *you* marry someone you'd met once at a ball and was more interested in your shoe-size than what you were like? How stupid is that?

Jade and Shelley left me alone. I think they

were so amazed that I hadn't kissed Darren that they couldn't think of anything to say. And when Joe came back to school, he found me in the playground and said he was *glad* I hadn't.

'Why?' I asked.

'Because he's such a big-head. He thinks all the girls adore him. It'll do him good to know that *you* don't at any rate.'

'Oh,' I said, surprised that he thought Darren would care.

'By the way,' added Joe, 'would you have kissed *me?*'

'Yes,' I said, blushing. 'Yes. That would've been OK.'

'Oh good,' said Joe and hobbled off to join his friends.

The rest of term seemed to fly by. Daisy and I couldn't wait for the start of the holidays. Last year, we weren't friends. Neither of us had a special friend then. Now we had loads of plans, mostly involving my tent which I'd put away while I was busy with *Cinderella*. I was *so* disappointed when I woke up on the first morning and it was pouring with rain.

'You can still use your tent,' Mum said, spotting how glum I looked over breakfast. 'When people go camping, it often rains. Put on your waterproofs. It won't take long to put it up.'

It took Daisy and me ages. It hadn't rained for weeks and the ground was rock hard. By the time we'd got the tent up, we were like drowned rats and couldn't wait to get back inside the house. All we wanted to do was have hot showers and curl up in front of the television.

But Mum wouldn't let us. 'No way,' she said. 'Having showers is fine but frittering away the first day of the holidays watching TV is not. No, we'll lend Daisy a bathrobe and you can set up a beauty parlour. You can borrow my make-up and nail varnish and really pamper yourselves. I'll bring you some hot chocolate when you're ready.'

My eyes lit up. Mum never lets me borrow her

make-up and nail varnish. She must have been feeling really sorry for us. We've never played beauty parlours. It sounded like fun.

'Would you like to visit our beauty parlour later?' I asked Mum. 'We could give you a manatee.'

'A manatee?' said Mum. 'Isn't that some sort of seal?'

'She means a manicure,' said Daisy, laughing. 'Will you come?'

'I think I'll be free at about twelve o'clock,' said Mum. 'Would that suit you?'

'I'm sure we can squeeze you in,' I said. 'Would you like an appointment card, Madam?'

'No, I can remember, thanks,' said Mum. 'Bye for now.'

I found an old bathrobe while Daisy had her shower. She's a bit smaller than me, so it fitted.

'Ooh, this is lovely,' she said when she'd snuggled into it. 'I've never had a bathrobe.'

'You can have it, if you like,' I said. 'It was only going to a charity shop.'

'Ooh, can I?' said Daisy. 'That'd be lovely. I use an old jumper of my mum's at the moment.'

That was odd, I thought, as I stood under the shower. Could Daisy mean she didn't have a dressing gown? Suddenly, I was embarrassed, thinking of all the times we'd tried on things from my wardrobe when, meanwhile, Daisy was using an old jumper for a dressing gown! All the fun of the beauty salon game seemed to vanish. What had I been thinking? Call myself a saint-in-training? Dream on! Saints didn't have wardrobes crammed with clothes, saints didn't have bathrobes and dressing gowns, saints wore simple clothes and slept on straw. They gave away anything they didn't need. I couldn't imagine St Clare of Assisi or St Teresa of Avila sitting around doing their nails! What a waste of time and money they'd think that was! St Clare had founded an order of nuns called the Poor Clares because they lived so simply and St Teresa's nuns were called the 'barefoot' Carmelites because they wore sandals instead of shoes!

'I don't think I want to play beauty salons any more,' I said to Daisy, as I sipped the hot chocolate Mum had made. 'I'd rather play "saints". We haven't played that for ages.'

'Which saint?' said Daisy.

'Oh, I don't know. Someone quiet and simple, I suppose. Someone we haven't done before.'

'Sounds a bit boring,' said Daisy. 'I'd rather play beauty salons.'

'I don't think saints do beauty salons,' I said. 'And I *am* still a saint-in-training. I don't think saints were really into beauty.'

'Of course they were,' said Daisy. 'Look at St Francis! He thought the world was fantastically beautiful.'

'I don't mean that sort of beauty,' I said crossly. 'I mean putting on make-up and doing your hair. St Clare cut *off* her hair to show that she didn't want to be married, she wanted to devote her life to God. And St Catherine of Siena did too.'

Daisy's eyes gleamed. 'I've always wanted to

cut off my hair,' she said. 'Mum likes me to keep it long but it's such a nuisance. She trims it every so often to stop it getting split ends but I'd much rather it was short.'

I looked at her hair. Her bunches didn't suit her; they just made her plump, guinea-pig cheeks look even fatter.

'Would you like me to cut it?' I said. 'I'm sure I could do it in a bob like mine.'

'Ooh yes,' said Daisy. 'It is my hair, after all.'

'Your mum might be cross,' I said.

'I don't care,' said Daisy. 'I'm fed up with it. I've always had my hair like this. I want a change.'

'OK, then,' I said. 'I'll find some scissors.'

I rummaged through my pencil case and quickly found a pair.

'They're not very big,' I said. 'Do you think that matters?'

'I don't see why it should,' said Daisy, pulling out her bobbles. 'Come on. Let's get going. I can't wait.'

Daisy brushed her hair through. It had kinks in

both sides where the bobbles had been. If she was going to have a smooth, shiny bob like mine, I'd have to get rid of those. I brushed it through again. It was thick and bouncy. It didn't feel like mine at all.

'What's the matter?' asked Daisy. 'Aren't you going to start?'

'Oh yes,' I said. 'I'm just giving it a good brushing. Won't be a minute.'

Five minutes later, Daisy's hair still wouldn't hang straight. The kinks from the bobbles seemed to be there for life.

'What are you waiting for?' asked Daisy. 'Don't worry if it's a bit wavy. My hair always is. Just cut it!'

'Oh all right then,' I said. I combed down a section of hair, just as I thought the hairdresser did. Snip! A hank of it fell to the floor. I looked at the cut ends. They didn't seem quite straight but I thought I could check it over when I'd finished. I picked up another section and cut again. Hmm. Not bad. Carefully I worked my way round to the back of Daisy's head. Here, it got harder. I'd never realized before but Daisy has really thick, springy hair. At the back, it was ever so difficult to cut with my little scissors.

'I'll have to find some sharper scissors,' I said. 'Won't be a minute!' Then I raced off to get Mum's sewing scissors from her workbasket.

'Is that you, Jenni?' called Mum. 'How's the beauty parlour?'

'Oh fine,' I shouted back. 'I'm just doing Daisy's hair.'

'Don't forget my appointment,' she called back.

I *had* forgotten. I'd have to hurry. What a surprise she would have when she came up and saw Daisy's new hairstyle!

'I'll have to speed up,' I said to Daisy. 'Mum's coming up at twelve, remember.' I combed Daisy's hair again and snipped. It was so much easier with the new scissors! Halo loved it. She kept leaping up to catch the hair as it floated to the ground. When I'd finished, I stood back to survey

my handiwork and – oh no! – the hair on one side of Daisy's face was shorter than on the other!

'What's wrong?' asked Daisy.

'Oh nothing,' I said, trying not to panic. 'It's just a bit uneven, that's all. It'll be easy to tidy up with these sharp scissors.'

But it wasn't. However hard I tried, I couldn't get the two sides the same length. They were getting shorter and shorter and the back was still quite long. I decided I'd better sort that out before I went any further. But the shorter I cut Daisy's hair, the more it wanted to stick out. It seemed to have grown springs! I couldn't understand why it wouldn't hang straight like mine does. It wasn't as if it was curly.

'Gosh,' said Daisy. 'It's taking a long time.'

'I know,' I said. 'But then I don't do it every day like a proper hairdresser.'

'Never mind,' said Daisy. 'It'll be worth it.'

I looked at what I'd done and wished I could agree. Daisy's hair looked like a monk's without the bald bit in the middle. She had a short, bushy ring all round her head. I knew that people had something called layers put in their hair when it was very thick but I didn't know how to do them. What was Daisy going to say when she saw what I'd done? She had been so excited and was going to be so disappointed! I stared at all the hair lying on the floor. If only I could stick some of it back!

Just then, Mum arrived.

'Hello,' she said, pushing open the door. 'Is it time for my... Jenni, what on earth are you doing?'

I stood back miserably. 'Making a mess,' I said. 'I'm really sorry, Daisy.' Then I burst into tears.

Slowly, Daisy got up and opened my wardrobe door. There's a mirror on the back of it.

'Oh no!' she said, looking at her reflection. 'Oh no! My mum's going to go ballistic!' Then she burst into tears too.

When we'd both stopped crying all over Mum, she made us wash our faces and took us downstairs. She didn't tell me off. She must have known I didn't need anyone to tell me how stupid I'd been. She made a pot of tea and put some chocolate biscuits on the table but I didn't feel like eating them. I just sat there, cuddling Halo.

'There's only one thing to do,' said Mum. 'Daisy will have to have a proper haircut. There's enough left for a nice, neat cropped style. I think it should suit her rather well.'

At this, Daisy gave a huge great shuddering sob and yet more tears rolled down her face.

'We can't afford it,' she whispered. 'That's why I keep my hair long. That way Mum can just trim it every so often.'

I gaped at Daisy. Couldn't afford to have her hair cut? Then I realized how dense I was being. It wasn't all that long ago that Jade and Shelley were making fun of Daisy for wearing Teletubbies knickers.* I'd tried to sell the church brasses to make some money to buy some new ones for her. It had all gone terribly wrong and since then I'd rather forgotten that because

* See *Saint Jenni: Super Hero*

77

Daisy's mum is poorly, she can't work.

Mum put her arm round Daisy. 'In that case,' she said, 'I'll take you myself and pay for it. It's my fault it's happened. I should have been keeping an eye on you better.'

'You can't do that!' said Daisy. 'Mum would be so embarrassed!'

'Daisy,' said Mum gently. 'I don't really think there's much choice. I'll give your mum a ring and sort it out.'

It took a while. Daisy was right. Her mum was very upset, not just about what I'd done but about Mum paying for a proper cut. At last, we went off to the salon. I didn't want to go but I felt I ought to. A saint has to be brave, even in the most difficult situations.

'Oh dear,' said the hairdresser to Daisy. 'Did you do this yourself, love?'

'No, it was me,' I said, in a small voice. 'She wanted it like mine.'

The hairdresser was very nice about it. He

explained that Daisy's hair was totally unlike mine and needed a completely different sort of cut. 'It's very springy and strong,' he said, 'but I think we can come up with something that will look quite good.'

He was right. By the time he'd finished, Daisy was transformed. She didn't look at all like a guinea-pig any more.

'Gosh,' said Mum. 'You look great. Very stylish, very feisty. I'm sure I shouldn't say this, but that hairstyle would look really good with a stud in your nose!'

'Maybe when I'm older,' said Daisy. She couldn't take her eyes off her reflection in the mirror.

'Do you like it then?' I said.

Daisy grinned at me. 'It's brilliant,' she said, 'but Mum'll still go bananas.'

6

Call yourself a saint?

I didn't enjoy taking Daisy home. It was the first time I'd been there and the first time I'd met her mum. They lived in a tiny flat. It was spotlessly clean, just like Daisy's clothes always were, but it seemed terribly bare. Daisy took me into her bedroom while the mums talked and I was so embarrassed I wanted to curl up and die. I thought of all the times I'd talked to Daisy about how unsuitable my room was for a trainee saint and how it ought to be small and bare with nothing much more than a bed. Well, that was just how Daisy's room was. Instead of a wardrobe, she had a rail fastened across the corner where her tiny collection of clothes hung – her school uniform, a couple of pairs of trousers and a few tops. I thought of my crammed wardrobe and felt sick.

Daisy's mum was very polite, telling me how pleased Daisy was with her new hairstyle. I just kept thinking how awful it was to know that a really short cut suited you but that you might not be able to keep it like that. Daisy's mum walked with great difficulty and I thought how hard it must be for her to look after herself and Daisy. And I'd made things worse.

I cried all the way home.

'Come on, Jenni,' said Mum. 'It's not the end of the world. Daisy's mum is getting used to the idea.'

'That's not the point,' I mumbled.

Mum sighed. 'Why don't you go and have a chat with Mrs Brindley?' she suggested. 'She usually manages to cheer you up.'

I shook my head and scooped up Halo who was winding herself round my legs. I hadn't thought about Daisy's mum's point of view at all.

I hadn't really thought about Daisy's. I'd just thought about mine. Really I had wanted to play at beauty parlours and 'saints' at the same time and cutting Daisy's hair had meant I could. I didn't want to tell Mrs Brindley.

'Well, go and see if the vicar wants a bit of help in his garden, then,' said Mum. 'That might make you feel better.'

I nodded. It would. If I did something useful for the vicar, maybe I wouldn't feel quite such a toad. I set down Halo but she followed me out of the door. She always knows when I'm upset.

The vicar was already working in his garden. His wife sent me out to find him.

I hurried round the side of the house and down to the vegetable patch, Halo skipping along beside me.

'Why, hello Jenni!' said the vicar. 'You're just the person I need! Fancy doing some weeding?'

I nodded. 'I've done something terrible,' I blurted out.

'What, worse than eating all my strawberries?' he asked with a smile. 'Worse than trying to burgle the church?'

'Much, much worse,' I said.

'Tell me all about it then,' said the vicar.

Half an hour and a huge heap of weeds later, I felt much better. The vicar didn't say much; mostly he just listened. He was like one of the quiet, chilled-out saints really. Maybe that's why people liked to visit them – not because they said anything great but just because they listened.

After tea I told Mum I was going to tidy out my room.

'Are you sure, love?' she said. 'Aren't you a bit tired?'

I *was* tired but I didn't think I could sleep until I'd done something about my room. I knew now that I didn't want it to be as bare and simple as Daisy's – it was silly to think that I ever would, even if I did grow up to be a saint – but I also knew that I didn't need half the stuff I had.

There were clothes I'd hardly worn and books and toys that I'd only looked at a couple of times. I made a huge heap in the middle of my room. It wasn't difficult once I'd got going. Just thinking about Daisy's bare room made it quite easy. Not dead easy. But easy enough. Finally, I picked up my *Big Book of Saints* from where it was lying by my bed. I'd read it several times, from cover to cover, and knew most of the stories almost by heart. I didn't really need it any more so I ought to give it away. Carefully, I laid it down beside everything else.

When Mum came to tell me it was bed-time, she was amazed by how much I'd done.

'Wow, Jenni!' she said. 'Looks like a trip to the charity shop tomorrow!'

'No,' I said. 'All this is for Daisy.'

Mum looked worried. 'Are you sure she'll want it?' she asked.

'Want it? Of course she'll want it!' I said. 'Mum, you should see her bedroom. She's got *nothing.*'

'Some people are quite happy with nothing much at all,' said Mum.

'Like who?' I demanded.

'Like saints,' said Mum.

'You don't know anything about saints,' I blustered, going red because she was right.

'Oh yes I do!' she retorted. 'You can't live with a trainee saint for months without learning something about them!'

'Well, Daisy isn't a saint,' I argued. 'She's just ordinary. She's bound to want all this stuff.'

'*You* don't,' said Mum.

'Yes, but I've got loads of other stuff. Daisy hasn't.'

'Maybe Daisy doesn't want...' Mum stopped. 'Oh never mind. We're going round in circles. Do what you think is best.'

The next day, Daisy came round in the afternoon. We were going to have tea together and then Dad was taking us swimming. The sun had come out so we could play in the tent but I couldn't wait to show Daisy all the stuff I'd got for her. I dragged her up the stairs.

'I've got this great surprise for you, Daisy,' I told her. 'Come and see!'

I flung open the door of my room. 'Look,' I said.

'Wow!' said Daisy. 'Where did all that come from?'

'Out of the cupboards, from under my bed, in boxes,' I said. 'And it's all for you!'

'It's all for me?' Daisy looked confused. 'Why?'

I gaped at her. Wasn't it obvious?

'Because you haven't got anything, of course! I felt so awful yesterday when I was in your flat – I was so embarrassed!'

'Embarrassed?' said Daisy, going red. 'Embarrassed to be in my flat?'

'No, no,' I tried to explain. 'I mean embarrassed that I'd gone on about living a simple life like a saint when you *have* to because you've got no money. So I thought I'd give you some of the stuff I don't need.' As soon as I'd finished, I realized

I'd said something terribly wrong. Daisy's face was almost purple.

'Fine!' exploded Daisy. 'Fine! Is that what you think saints do? Dump all their left-overs on their embarrassing little friends who live in grotty flats? Is that it?'

'No, no, that's not it at all,' I howled. 'I didn't mean it like that! I was trying to make up for wrecking your hair and upsetting your mum and everything!'

'Oh, so you think my hair's a wreck now, do you? So all that stuff you said yesterday about it suiting me was lies, was it? Well, I don't want a friend like you any more, *Saint* Jenni. You can go and practise being a saint on someone else!'

And Daisy stomped out of my room, ran down the stairs and out into the street.

I stood quite still, not knowing what on earth to do. What would Mrs Brindley say? What would the vicar say? What would a saint do?

I had no idea – but I knew what I *wanted* to do.

I snatched up Halo who was mewing in distress, and ran after Daisy.

I'm better at running than Daisy but I was carrying Halo.

'Daisy!' I shouted. 'Daisy, wait!'

Daisy looked over her shoulder and ran faster – so I ran faster too. My heart was pounding and my throat hurt but I was determined to catch her. She was slowing down, I could tell.

'Daisy,' I gasped. 'Daisy, I'm sorry! Please wait for me!'

Daisy stopped. She turned and faced me. Her face was so angry that I was shocked. She had changed a lot in the last few months.

'Well?' she demanded.

I thrust Halo into her arms. I needed my hands free because I was crying and wanted to wipe my nose.

'I didn't mean… I was just trying to be kind… I was trying to make up for… oh, it's so hard trying to be a saint,' I sobbed. 'And I just keep getting it wrong.'

'No, you don't,' said Daisy, suddenly looking fed-up instead of angry. 'Not all the time anyway. But you always think that being a saint is such a big thing – all about taming wild animals or being a super hero or something.'

'No, I don't. I'm trying to be a chilled-out saint at the moment,' I hiccuped, 'all calm and quiet and peaceful.'

Daisy started to laugh. 'Yes, but even then you've got to make it into something big – a cave on the lawn or giving me a huge pile of clothes and toys.'

'But the saints did big things,' I objected.

'Yes and that's why people tell stories about them. But you don't *have* to do big things to be saintly.'

'Well, I might as well give up,' I sighed, blowing my nose again. 'I can't even get it right for my best friend.'

'Rubbish,' said Daisy. 'That's total rubbish! Think what I was like a few months ago – always crying and scared stiff of going to school. If it wasn't for you, I'd still be like that. You made it all different.'

'How?' I demanded, baffled.

'Oh, just little things. Playing with me when no one else would, showing me how to do handstands, sticking up for me against Jade and Shelley, letting me come and play at your house even when I didn't invite you back, taking me swimming…'*

'Stop, stop,' I said, blushing. 'I'm not that nice really. You're forgetting about all the mean bits. Like when I made you be the red carpet when I was playing at being the queen and when I hit you when we were playing "saints".* Oh yes, and when I wouldn't speak to you after I hurt my head. You're making me sound like a… like a…'

'Saint?' asked Daisy, handing Halo back to me.

I smiled, rubbing my tears away. 'Well, yes. Maybe. And I'm not, am I? I've got a long way to go.'

Daisy shrugged. 'At least you try,' she said, 'even if it does go wrong.'

* See *Saint Jenni: Super Hero* and *Saint Jenni: Animal Crazy*

'So are you still my friend?' I asked. 'Even after…?'

'Forget it,' said Daisy. 'You were only trying to be kind. I'm just too proud.'

'Tut, tut,' I said, with a grin. 'Being proud isn't very saintly, you know.'

'I never said it was,' said Daisy. 'And you're the saint-in-training, not me. Now can we go back and look through all that stuff you're getting rid of, please? If you still want to give it to me, that is.'

'Of course I do,' I said. 'But if you don't mind, I'm going to hang on to my *Big Book of Saints*. I think I might still need it after all. What do you think, Halo?'

Halo snuggled against my chest and purred.

'She agrees,' I said.

'So do I,' said Daisy. 'But please can I borrow it sometime?'

'Of course you can,' I said, with a grin. 'Come on. All that running's made me thirsty. Let's go home.'

Jenni's Guide to the Saints

Part 3

Saints are amazing people who do acts of great kindness or bravery or holiness, because of their belief in God... hmm, sounds good to me!

St Cecilia

A brilliant musician – but a Roman governor still wanted to kill her for her faith in Jesus. It wasn't easy. First he tried to suffocate her in her bathroom. Then he tried to chop off her head – but she survived for three days and gave all her money to the poor!

St Dorothy

When a Roman governor sent two sisters to Dorothy to persuade her to give up her Christian faith, they became Christians too – so he burnt them to death and made Dorothy watch, before killing her as well! A man mockingly asked her to send flowers and fruit from heaven. And she did! Astonishing!

Hildegard of Bingen

A nun who wrote wonderful hymns but kept quiet about her visions from God – until he told her to speak out. She did exactly that, bravely telling kings and popes what they were doing wrong. Her books warned that people were destroying the earth – and that was a thousand years ago!

St Simeon the Stylite (stylos is the Greek word for pillar)

Simeon spent 37 years living on top of a pillar so that he could think and pray. He gradually built taller pillars because people would keep talking to him! The last was 18 metres high and his food was sent up by pulley. Not that he ate much! Sometimes he spoke to his visitors but mostly he prayed. Mind-boggling!

St Teresa of Avila

Teresa was packed off to school when her mother died. She went a bit wild but later got ill and realized how bad she'd been so she became a nun. She was so shocked by the other nuns' behaviour that she began the order of 'barefoot' Carmelite nuns who lived very simply indeed.

St Frideswide (pronounced Freedeswider)

The king really fancied Frideswide but she only wanted to serve God. The king got nasty about it and chased her through a forest where a branch snapped back in his face and blinded him.

Frideswide hid in Oxford, forgave the king and prayed that his sight would come back – which it did!

St Winifride

Winifride was very pure and holy and wanted nothing to do with Prince Caradoc. She ran to a church to escape him – but he cut off her head! Her uncle prayed to God – and she came back to life! A fountain of healing water sprang up where she fell. Pity Caradoc didn't drown in it!

For St Cuthbert, St Sergius and St Francis of Assisi see *Saint Jenni: Animal Crazy*.

For St Paul, St Catherine of Alexandria and St Clare of Assisi see *Saint Jenni: Super Hero*.